The
Seventh Candle

And other Folk Tales
Of Eastern Europe

The Seventh Candle

And other Folk Tales
Of Eastern Europe

by David Einhorn

translated from the Yiddish by Gertrude Pashin

Nov 1970

illustrated by Ezekiel Schloss

Ktav Publishing House, Inc.

LIBRARY OF CONGRESS CATALOG CARD NUMBER: 68-10968
MANUFACTURED IN THE UNITED STATES OF AMERICA

TABLE OF CONTENTS

The Synagogue That Wept

ONCE upon a time, in a little Jewish town hidden away among huge pine forests, there was an old, old synagogue. It was a frame building and so old, it was no longer used as a house of worship. The door was shut and it stood forsaken and alone. Thick grass grew among the stone steps and swallows built their nests underneath its sagging roof. And all about and around the neighboring towns it was known as "The Weeping Synagogue." It was said that after midnight when all pious Jews arose to mourn the destruction of the Temple, sounds could be heard from behind the closed door; sounds of drops, drops like tears falling, and someone inside quietly weeping.

Old grandfathers would tell the story of the synagogue.

Hundreds of years ago, a very learned rabbi lived in this little town. He was famed for his piety throughout the land. This rabbi was very, very poor and he lived in a little house not far from the synagogue. He studied the Torah continuously, and even late at night when all the town was asleep, he would sit alone in the big dark synagogue absorbed in a book, reading by the light of a candle.

Once, after midnight, while sitting all alone in the synagogue, the rabbi heard a voice from the Holy Ark saying, "Because of your piety and righteousness, you have earned great favor in Heaven. The moment for your reward is now at hand. Make a wish and it shall be granted. But hurry, for time is short."

And the rabbi thought: "What shall I wish for? Wealth leads to sin. Power leads to terror. Honor makes one despise another. Wisdom? The greatest wisdom of all is in the Torah, and I study that day and night. No," he quietly said, "I have nothing to wish for."

Then a sound of weeping came from the Holy Ark and a voice said, "You wretched man! You thought only of yourself. You might have wished for the coming of the Messiah and the salvation of the world."

When the sexton arrived at the synagogue in the morning, he found the rabbi lying unconscious on the floor at the foot of the Holy Ark. He was quickly revived and taken to his little house. The rabbi then asked that the oldest and most pious Jews of the community be brought before him. He told them what had happened in the synagogue during the night and then he died.

At night, when the sexton approached the door of the synagogue, he heard a silent weeping from within. And since then, every night after midnight, from behind the door sounds can be heard; sounds as of tear drops falling from the ceiling. This was the synagogue weeping for the golden moment that had been lost.

The Seventh Candle

IN an old castle in Poland there once lived a duke who was a very lonely man. His castle was deep in the woods, surrounded by forests of birch and pine trees. Horses and hunting were all the duke cared about. He might be seen at any time of the day or night galloping through the dark woods on his black horse. His rifle and his hunting dogs were always with him.

Not too far away from the castle there was a wayside inn

wherein there dwelt a Jew, his wife and their little boy. They lived quietly and worked hard all week.

On Fridays the wife prepared for the Sabbath. She cleaned her home thoroughly, covered the table with a snow-white cloth and placed seven candles on it. She lighted four candles in honor of the Sabbath and the other three for herself, her husband and her child. Covering her face with her hands, she prayed, "Lord of the Universe, the holy Sabbath approaches, the day of peace and tranquillity for all mankind. Consecrate my home by these lights which I now kindle. Bless my home with peace and happiness; bless my husband, my child and all Jews. Amen."

In her heart, the mother prayed for her son most of all. And indeed, the boy was a most remarkable child. He was not only beautiful, good and very bright but also played the violin brilliantly. He played with such sweetness of expression that passersby would stop to listen in wonder.

One time the Polish nobleman, riding on his black horse, passed the inn and heard the wonderful music. Enchanted by the playing, he dismounted from his horse, walked to the window and saw the child playing. "This boy shall be my heir," the duke said to himself. He remounted his horse and rode back to his castle.

On the following morning the duke came to the inn, accompanied by his armed soldiers. "Sell me your child," he commanded the innkeeper.

The father was terrified. "Even if you fill this entire house with gold," he cried, "I will not give you my son. He is dearer to me than life itself."

"Then I shall take him from you by force," the duke replied. "The lives of my subjects are my property." And in spite of the tears and pleas of the desperate parents, the duke put the little boy on his horse and rode away with him.

Soon thereafter the heartbroken parents left the inn and moved to a nearby town.

Years rolled by. The duke raised the child as his own son. He sent him to the capital city where he attended the finest schools. The boy lived like a prince in a palace surrounded by very luxury. As he grew up he forgot all about his parents.

His poor mother, however, could not forget her son. She lighted the same seven candles every Friday night and offered the same prayer. But the flame on the seventh candle always burned with a weak and dim light.

At last the duke died and willed all his possessions and his title to the boy. According to custom the young duke went to visit the lands he had inherited.

It was Friday evening when the young nobleman arrived in the town where his parents lived. The entire town seemed to be under the spell of the peace and quiet of the Sabbath. From every window shone the lights of the Sabbath candles.

In one of the windows of a little house the duke noticed seven lights. As he looked, the seventh light grew brighter and brighter, until it shone with such radiance that he had to shut his eyes. He suddenly remembered his youth, his father and his mother. As in a trance he approached the door of his parents home. His old mother was on the doorstep and she embraced him with tears in her eyes.

"I knew you were here," she quietly said. "Your light began to shine brightly."

The young duke visited with his parents all that Sabbath. A short time after that he sold all his properties and took his parents with him to Amsterdam. There he returned to his Jewish faith and became a famous violinist.

His mother, as was her custom, lighted seven candles every Friday night, but the flame of the seventh candle always shone brighter than all the rest.

IN a synagogue of a small Jewish community in Southern Russia, hung a "Ner Tamid," an Eternal Light. The members of the community guarded this light with a very special devotion and never allowed its brightness to grow dim. It burned constantly, and spread its soft glow throughout the darkened shadows of the synagogue.

The lamp was made of copper and was decorated with beautiful oriental engravings of flowers and leaves. Interlaced among these engravings were the words "Ner Tamid," "Eternal Light."

This lamp, according to legend, had been brought from Babylon hundreds and hundreds of years ago by Jewish travelers. They had come to this little town in southern Russia after many wanderings. All they had with them was a Torah and this copper lamp.

Centuries later, a tyrant by the name of Bogdan Chmielnitzki rose to power. He gathered about him hordes of bandits who spread terror and destruction wherever they went. When they came into a Jewish town they would murder many of its inhabitants, and sell the others as slaves to the Turks.

This particular community suffered the same fate as others that had been visited by this gang of desperados. It fell before the tyrant and his mob. Several days after the disaster, a peasant came to the devastated town to look for loot among its ruins. While digging in the ashes of the synagogue, he found the lamp, complete and undamaged, its light still softly glowing.

The peasant took the lamp home with him and hung it in front of his sacred pictures. The pictures suddenly seemed to disappear from his sight. All he could see was the gentle glow from the lamp.

"Throw the lamp into the oven," his wife said. "It is bewitched."

The peasant threw the lamp into the blazing fire of the oven. But wonder of wonders! The flames in the oven were smothered but the lamp still kept shining with its mellow light.

"Throw it into the water," again urged his wife. "The water will douse the flame." The peasant threw the lamp into the

11

stream that ran past his hut.

That night when he went to draw water, he noticed the lamp at the bottom of the stream. Its little flame was still burning, casting a silvery light upon the surface of the water. The peasant was overcome by a nameless fear. He pulled the lamp out of the water and carried it far, far into the deep forest. There he hung it on a branch of a tall tree. The branches quickly enfolded the lamp, covered it with their leaves and hid it from sight.

And so a very long time passed.

Many years later, a group of Jews who had been freed from their slavery were returning home to the little town in the southern part of Russia. While walking through the woods at night they noticed a faint light from between the branches of a tree. One of the men climbed the tree to see what it might be. Much to his amazement he found the old copper "Ner Tamid."

As soon as they reached home the Jews rebuilt the synagogue. The lamp was hung reverently in its place. At that moment the little flame began to flicker and grow smaller and smaller as though it were about to die out.

"From now on it shall be your duty," the rabbi said, "to preserve this lamp and protect its flame. Keep it filled with oil always, and forever guard its light."

And now once again the lamp burns constantly and spreads its soft light throughout the darkened shadows of the synagogue, just as it had done so very long, long ago.

The Fruit of the Holy Land

IT was a small green palm tree and it had graced the home of the old rabbi. When the rabbi went to the Holy Land he took the plant with him. No one knows what happened to the little palm in the Holy Land, but for generations the story of this wonderful little palm was told and retold by fathers to their children.

Many long years ago, a poor widow and her ten year old little boy whose name was Moishele lived in this town. The widow trudged all day long from door to door selling eggs and vegetables which she carried in two baskets. When night fell she returned home to her little house and to Moishele, her only comfort. Moishele waited for her at the window, gazing at the blue evening sky.

"What are you dreaming about, my child?" the widow asked as she lighted the stove and prepared supper.

"I am thinking of all that I learned in *heder* today," Moishele answered. "Tell me, mother, have you ever seen all those wonderful fruits we read about in the sacred books? Have you ever seen dates and grapes, figs and oranges?"

"No," the mother replied. "How could I see such fruits? We live in a cold climate. These fruits grow on the hills of the Jordan in the Holy Land where the weather is always warm."

"I want to see them," Moishele stubbornly insisted.

It was sometime during the latter part of January when Moishele became very ill. He was running a very high fever. His desperate mother put him to bed and sat down beside him. The weather was so bitterly cold that the log dwellings crackled from the frost. An angry snowstorm raged across the town and howled in the chimneys with the sound of a hundred wolves.

"Mama," Moishele cried feverishly, "bring me grapes. Bring me dates and figs and oranges. I want to see them all. I want to eat them."

"How can I do that for you, dear child?" the mother asked with tears in her eyes. "The Holy Land is so far, so very far away!"

At that moment there was a knock on the door. When the mother opened the door she saw before her an old man with a long white beard. He carried a sack upon his back and held a heavy cane in his hand.

"Good woman," said the old man, "I have come a long, long way and I am very tired. All doors seem to be closed. Would you put me up for the night?"

"Come in," the widow invited him with a friendly gesture. "You will find a warm place near the stove and you can spend the night here."

The old man brushed the snow from himself and went into the house. He sat down quietly in a corner near the stove.

"Mama," again begged Moishele, "Give me grapes and dates and figs and oranges. I want to see them and I want to taste them."

The old man rose from his chair. He took his sack and brought it to Moishele's bed. Opening the sack, he took out a fresh bunch of pale green grapes with the dew still on them and said, "Here you are, my child. Recite the blessing and eat. I have just brought these from the Holy Land." He then took out a luscious green fig webbed with little purple veins, some dates and a ripe orange.

Moishele sat up and for a long time stared with his big black eyes at the wonderful fruits. He recited the blessing and began to eat. When Moishele finished eating all the fruit, the old man disappeared with his sack and his cane.

"It was the Prophet Elijah," the mother murmured as she neared the bed. Moishele was sleeping peacefully. The fever had left him and in his open hand he held the pit of a date.

The following day the widow told the rabbi about the remarkable incident. The rabbi examined the pit and said, "Plant this pit and let it grow. Keep it as a remembrance of the miracle."

Moishele grew up and later became a very famous rabbi. All of his life he watched over this palm that had grown from the pit of a date. And one day he returned this palm to the Holy Land.

A Visit with Abraham

ONCE, long, long ago, there was a very pious and very learned rabbi. He had great compassion for his fellow Jews and wished to share their sorrows with them. And so he became a homeless wanderer traveling about the country. For several years the great rabbi walked from town to town with a sack upon his back and a heavy walking stick in his hand. He never rested at night where he passed the day.

One time the rabbi stopped at a Jewish roadside inn, where he met another traveler. This traveler was an old man, sitting with his sack and his cane at his side, reading from a book.

After they greeted each other, the stranger said to the rabbi, "You do not help nor do you serve your people by being an exile and wandering from place to place. I have just come from a different part of the country. In that region there is a community that is very poor. The people have neither a rabbi nor an instructor. They may, God forbid, forget our Torah. Go to them. Be their rabbi and their teacher."

The rabbi quickly took his leave from the stranger. He picked up his sack, and taking his walking stick, left the inn.

"Keep going south," the old man called after him. "God will guide you there."

The rabbi started on his journey, but lost his way in the wilderness of a dense forest. He wandered all week through the woods, always bearing south. He stilled his hunger with the wild fruits, blackberries and mushrooms that he found in the forest, and quenched his thirst with the waters from the streams.

On Friday evening the rabbi stopped under an old oak tree. He placed his sack on the soft moss and prepared for his Sabbath rest. Looking about, he noticed a light shining through the trees and he walked towards it. When he neared the light he saw before him a stretch of land, green and broad. In the center of this area stood a beautiful palace of white marble, with all its windows shining like jewels. A stately old man waited at the gate and he extended his hand in welcome as the rabbi approached.

"Blessed be thou in this house of mine," the old man said. "This Sabbath you shall rest here, in my home."

The aged man took the rabbi by the arm and entrusted him to a servant whom he called "Eliezer." The servant addressed the old man as "Rabbi Abraham."

The servant led the rabbi to a pool made of white alabaster. It was filled with water that reflected the most marvelous light. The rabbi bathed in this radiance. The servant then brought him garments of white silk and conducted him to a beautiful bright room where the aged man was sitting. As the rabbi entered, the old man rose from his chair and went with him to the synagogue which was situated in the middle of a garden.

The walls of this synagogue were encrusted with diamonds and precious stones. They glittered and sparkled with every color in the rainbow. The synagogue was filled with venerable ancients, all dressed in white. After greeting the rabbi, they all stood up for prayers. The cantor was called David and the others bore the names Adam, Enoch, Abraham, Isaac, Joseph, Moses, Solomon, and Elijah.

The rabbi spent all that Sabbath day in the palace. Rabbi Abraham studied with him and taught him the wonders and secrets of the Torah which no mortal had yet learned.

When the sun set Rabbi Abraham made the Havdallah benediction and blessed the rabbi. The servant took the rabbi by the hand, and in an instant he found himself in the market place of the town which he had been seeking.

The people of the community welcomed the rabbi with warmth and gladness and he began teaching the Torah to their children. This community later became a seat of great learning and many students of the rabbi became very famous scholars.

An Hour in Paradise

IN a small Jewish town there once lived a shoemaker with his wife and their two children. He was very poor. A little straw roofed hut and a goat were all he owned. From sunrise to sunset the shoemaker worked at his bench mending shoes for everyone in town. He never complained, however, and thanked God every day for his daily bread. A gay tune accompanied by the rhythmic beat of his hammer could always be heard from his open window.

One day, a man, tall and slender, entered the shoemaker's hut. He had blue eyes that were cold and piercing and was dressed like a rich Polish nobleman.

"I need a shoemaker on my estate," stated the nobleman, "I like you. If you will move to my principality I shall give you a fine home, a field and a cow, a servant and a thousand gold coins a year."

"Are there any Jews in that region?" asked the shoemaker.

"No," replied the Polish count.

"In that case, I prefer to remain here," the shoemaker said.

The nobleman persisted and offered him more money, but the shoemaker stubbornly refused to accept any offer.

"What is it you want me to give you for your services?" the Pole shouted angrily.

"An hour in Paradise," answered the shoemaker.

The count was furious. He ran out of the hut, slamming the door behind him.

The shoemaker and his family were very busy the following day beautifying their home for the holiday of Shavouth. They decorated the naked walls with green twigs and covered the floor with green grasses. After a festive supper the family went to bed.

In his sleep the shoemaker dreamt that an old man with a white beard spoke to him saying, "Go quickly to the window and look at the sky. It is about to split. Make a wish and it shall be granted."

The shoemaker rose from his bed and went to the window. A threadlike blue ray streaked across the sky and divided it into two halves. "An hour in Paradise!" the shoemaker called out.

The little hut was suddenly filled with light. Beautifully shaped leaves covered the twigs from which rare fruits hung. Birds of many colors flitted about, singing sweetly. The family woke up and sat spellbound listening to the song of the birds. An hour later everything vanished. All that was left of that shining hour was a handful of Paradise leaves on the bed where the children slept. The leaves had a most wonderful fragrance. The shoemaker's wife gathered them up and saved them.

Some time after that an epidemic among the children broke out in town. The shoemaker's children became very ill. "I will give them a whiff of those wonderful leaves. Maybe it will help them," thought the mother. She brought the leaves to the children and as soon as they inhaled their fragrance they became well. News of the healing power of the wonderful leaves soon spread throughout the town. All the sick children smelled their fragrance and were cured.

The story about the remarkable Paradise leaves finally reached the palace where the count who owned this territory lived. His only child had also fallen victim to the epidemic and was about to die. The count sent for the shoemaker and the wonderful leaves. The child inhaled their fragrance and was restored to health.

The count was so grateful to the shoemaker for the gift of his child's life that he presented him with a deed to the entire town. And the shoemaker with his wife and children lived happily in this little town the rest of their lives.

FAR, far away in a remote corner
of the unending plains in Southern Russia, lived a Jewish farmer
and his wife. They were simple people who worked very hard
all year. They cultivated their land and served God with devotion just as they had seen their parents do. Twice a year, on Passover and on Rosh Hashonah they traveled to a Jewish town in
order to spend the holidays among Jews.

While attending services at the synagogue one Passover, the countryman and his wife listened to a sermon delivered by a visiting preacher. He spoke about the customs of the Jewish people when they were a nation in the Holy Land. It was traditional at that time to offer sheaves of cuttings from the first yield of their fields as a gift to God.

After the holiday, when the couple returned to the farm, the wife said to her husband, "Why should we not do as our ancestors did in the Holy Land? The earth and everything in it belongs to God, the Creator. He makes bread grow everywhere. Let us set aside a piece of land for Him."

"Let it be as you wish," agreed the husband.

The next morning they selected a plot. They tilled the soil and planted wheat. And God's blessing truly shone upon this portion of the land. Here the wheat grew quickly. While green shoots still hugged the ground in the fields, tall ripe wheat, like brown gold, billowed across this spot.

The farmer and his wife reaped the crop. They tied the wheat into sheaves and divided the yield into three parts. The first portion they dedicated as a gift to God. From this wheat they baked Hallah for the Sabbath. The second portion they distributed among the poor and the third portion they saved and used as seed for planting. This became a ritual with them and they observed this custom year in and year out.

One Thursday evening a famous rabbi rode past the farmer's house. He was a long way from his destination and was afraid that he would be unable to reach it before the Sabbath. He therefore decided to spend the week end at the farmer's home. It happened to be during the time when the sacred wheat had ripened and the farmer and his wife went to gather the crop.

"Why do you reap the wheat so late at night?" the rabbi asked in surprise.

"This is consecrated wheat," replied the farmer, "and tomorrow we wish to bake the first loaves as a gift to God."

The rabbi looked at the devout couple sternly, and with anger in his voice said, "It is sinful to do so on alien soil when our Temple is destroyed."

The two poor souls became very frightened. They went to the field and set fire to the sheaves of wheat. That same night the rabbi's mind became a blank. He forgot everything he had studied and learned. In the morning a scorching sun arose and threatened the whole land with drought and hunger.

When the rabbi returned to his home town, he was met by the entire congregation. They begged him to pray for rain.

"I can no longer help you," said the rabbi. "Go to the farmer who lives two days' journey from here. Implore him to forgive me and ask him to pray for me and to pray for rain."

A delegation from the community was appointed to go to the farmer. When they related to him the rabbi's words, he went with his wife to the fire blackened field and prayed humbly and quietly, "Creator of the Universe, let these sheaves of burnt wheat be a sacrifice for us, for the rabbi and for the whole land. Accept this as a burnt offering and give us rain."

And so it was. Heavy clouds suddenly darkened the sky and rain, like a blessing, fell and watered all the fields of the land.

The Charred Wall

THE indescribable beauty of the old frame synagogue was known to all from near and far, and people came from everywhere to gaze in wonder at the magic of its art. It stood at one side of the small town not far from the river's edge, surrounded by a wide open space. Half its structure was sunk deep into the ground. The other half, with three roofs, one on top of the other, reached proudly towards the sky, high above all the other houses in town. One wall, however, was black, scorched by fire.

It was said that centuries ago, the Jews of this little town decided to build a synagogue. The wood for its construction was a gift from the count who owned this territory. He had ordered the finest trees from his own forests cut down for this purpose. When the interior of the synagogue was ready for painting and decorating, the elders of the community thought of a most remarkable craftsman called Shmuel, the Carpenter. Shmuel was a lonely and a very pious man who lived by himself on the other side of the town in a little house. Cherry, plum and apple trees grew all around it. He worked only half a day to earn his living and the other half he devoted to painting and carving all sorts of decorations on revered East Walls and Holy Arks. He adorned them with all sorts of wonderful flowers, trees and birds such as no one had ever seen before. The Jews believed that the Prophet Elijah had shown Shmuel a glimpse of the Garden of Eden and that he painted that which he had seen there.

When the elders of the community proposed that he decorate the synagogue, Shmuel was overjoyed and his happiness was complete. He asked for two years time in which to do it, and he worked at the synagogue tirelessly half the days and entire nights. He covered the walls and ceiling of the synagogue with green leaves on which colorful and exotic flowers bloomed. Entwined among these leaves and flowers were all manner of birds and beasts. On the East Wall he painted every musical instrument that had been used in the Temple. The Ark was carved so high up, that one's head had to be tilted far back in order to see the top. The engravings on both sides of the Ark were intricately interwoven with the figures of a lion, a leopard, a gazelle and an eagle. When the work was completed and the Jews came to see the synagogue, they could not believe that a mere mortal could have been the creator of so much beauty.

Several years later, on a hot windy summer night, fire broke out and flames engulfed the entire town. The Jewish population had but one thought in mind—the Torahs must be saved! They ran to the synagogue, and only after the Torahs were taken to safety did they themselves flee with their possessions to the opposite bank of the river. Shmuel, however, did not leave the synagogue. He alone remained. When the fire reached the synagogue and tongues of flame licked the tall windows, Shmuel, the Carpenter approached the Ark where a candle was burning, stuck his head inside and pleaded, "Lord of the Universe, You have given me the gift to create my own world; a world filled with love and beauty. I have used this gift to honor Your Name and to glorify Your House. If it is now Your will to destroy this synagogue by fire, let me perish with it."

The synagogue seemed to come alive at his words. The trees engraved on the walls and the ceiling began to sway and the birds began to sing mournfully. The harps and the violins harmonized in prayer, the lion roared, the gazelle wept and the leopard and the eagle howled bitterly. And at that moment a miracle occurred. The direction of the wind shifted and turned the flames away from the synagogue. When the Jews watching from the opposite side of the river saw this, they came with buckets of water and poured them on the smoldering wall.

Shmuel was found unconscious on the steps of the Holy Ark. He died the next day.

In time the Jews rebuilt their little town, but no houses were built near the synagogue.

On the ceiling of the synagogue, high above the altar, among those wonderful flowers and leaves, a tombstone is painted to perpetuate the memory of Shmuel, the Carpenter. Inscribed on it is his name, the day his work was finished, and the day he died.

The Last Recital

AFTER midnight on the ninth day of the Jewish month of Ab when pious Jews sit on the floor and lament the destruction of the Temple, two big tear drops, like two bright blue stars, fall from the heavens above. As they near the earth they break into thousands and thousands of brilliant sparks. When two such sparks fall into the eyes of a baby born that night, he is destined to become a great poet or musician. He will, however, never be joyful, for the pain of God's sorrow at the destruction of the Temple is felt in whatever he may create. And the ache touches the hearts of men with pity and compassion towards all who suffer.

During one such night on the Ninth day of Ab, a little boy was born to a penniless musician in a small Jewish town. Two bright, heavenly sparks fell into the eyes of this new born infant as soon as he opened them.

When the child grew older, his father made a little flute for him. It was made from the bark of a twig and had seven little holes in it. The little boy quickly learned to play on it. His music was sad and sweet, and had such an effect on people, that when enemies heard the music they clasped their hands in friendship and became friends. A wealthy man once happened to hear him play. He was so impressed with the boy's talent that he gave the father enough money to send his gifted son to a very fine conservatory to study music.

Years passed and the boy became a world famous violinist.

The young artist had many friends among the nobility. One of his friends, a count, invited him to play at a ball honoring his beautiful young daughter. The ball was to be held at the palace on the Ninth Day of Ab.

On his way to the count's palace the brilliant violinist was stopped by an old grey haired Jew, wearing a long coat. "Young man," said the Jew, "God's anguish flows through the strings of your violin. Do not debase this night with the gaiety of aliens."

The violinist was very young, and he quickly forgot the old

Jew and his words. He continued on to the palace and played for the guests. After the ball he went for a stroll in the palace gardens with the young countess. "Why does your violin always bring forth such heart-rending music that it makes one cry?" asked the countess.

"I do not know why, myself," replied the musician. "It is as though another hand, the hand of a stranger, were guiding mine and moving my fingers."

"Do try to play something gay for once," begged the countess. "Just for me."

The young artist took his violin and started to play dance music. Suddenly one of the strings on his violin snapped. The musician grew pale and fainted.

He was brought home to his father a short time later. He was very ill. For a year he sat near the window, silent and moody, never touching his violin.

On the Ninth Day of Ab, the night of Tisha B'Ab, the musician suddenly took his violin from the wall where it had been hanging and went to the old synagogue in town. As the Jews who were sitting on the floor began reciting the lamentations from the Book of Jeremiah, the gifted artist raised his violin, placed it in position and began to play. The melody he played was so sad and so beautiful that the entire congregation broke down and wept.

That very night the world famous young musician died. As a tribute to the memory of this great but unhappy artist, the congregation resolved that on the night of Tisha B'Ab the lamentations would hereafter be chanted with the tune of the melody he played on the last night of his life.

The Remarkable Water Carrier

ONCE upon a time a stranger came to a small town in Poland. He was a tall, broad shouldered man with a long, black beard and dark brooding eyes. He wore a tattered old sheepskin coat, a worn heavy looking fur hat and torn boots.

The stranger quietly entered the House of Worship, washed his hands and sat down near the door. No one knew who he was nor where he had come from. Silently he moved his lips and no one could tell whether he even knew the prayers. He lived from day to day on whatever the Jews from town brought him—a crust of black bread, potatoes or a bowl of soup. Personally, he asked for nothing.

A short time after the stranger arrived in town, the water carrier died. The Jews decided to give the job to the stranger. He worked faithfully all day long and kept the barrels filled with water. The townspeople gave him a slice of bread or a small coin in return for his services.

In this same town lived a very rich money lender. He was a miser and had no compassion for anyone who was poor. He cared only for gold and his greatest pleasure was to hoard it in an iron chest which he kept hidden in the cellar.

The shrewd money lender was quick to notice that the water carrier had no idea about the value of money. Instead of paying the carrier every day with a coin, the miser gave him an old button wrapped in a piece of paper. The water carrier would shove it into his pocket without a word.

One time this greedy man evicted a poor widow from her home because she owed him some money. It was on the day before Yom Kippur Eve and the widow had two small children, but this made no difference to the miser.

That night, when the town slept and all the lights were out, the water carrier came to the money lender's house and knocked at his door.

"Who is there?" asked the rich man.

"The water carrier," came the reply.

"What do you want?"

"You will soon find out," the water carrier said. And before the banker could get out of bed, the door opened of its own accord and the water carrier walked in.

"What do you want?" the rich man asked again.

"I want my wages for carrying water for you."

"I paid you every day," the money lender told him.

"That is true enough, but it is in your iron chest."

"That is impossible!" exclaimed the money lender.

The water carrier was firm. "Go down and see for yourself."

The tone in the water carrier's voice and the look in his eyes compelled the banker to do as he was told. He lighted a candle, and taking the key to his treasure, went down to the cellar without uttering another word. He opened the chest with shaking hands and to his amazement saw that all the pieces of paper with the buttons that he had given to the water carrier were indeed there, right on top. When he took them out he was horrified to find that the chest was filled with old buttons instead of gold.

The water carrier removed his paper wrappings by the light of the candle. Instead of old buttons, gold coins fell out. Taking a handful of coins, he handed them to the miser and said sharply, "This is for the widow. Now tear up her note."

The greedy man suddenly felt very guilty. He hung his head in shame, and obeyed. The water carrier left the moment the note was destroyed, and the miser saw that the iron chest was again filled with coins, brand new coins.

There was a great deal of excitement in town that morning. The money lender had come to the rabbi, bringing with him a bag full of gold. He asked that this gold be distributed among the poor.

The water carrier vanished from town that day. And just as no one knew where he had come from, no one ever knew where he had gone.

The Flying Letters

ONCE, long ago, in legendary times, there were two Jewish communities. The first community was ruled by a devilish tyrant who hated all men, especially the Jews. He issued a decree confiscating all the books in the Jewish community and ordered them burnt. He forbade the Jews, under penalty of death, to write or copy any religious works.

The Jews of this community, however, were very devout and very learned. They knew the Torah by heart and continued to teach it to their children by word of mouth. In order that the ritual of taking the scrolls from the Ark should not be forgotten, they fashioned a blank piece of parchment the exact length and width of a scroll, and a blind man who was very learned recited the portion for the week, as if he could see the written words.

The second community lived under the rule of a king that was kind and just. They enjoyed equal rights and privileges with the rest of the population. But the Jews in this community quickly forgot their Torah. Their synagogue remained closed even on the Sabbath. Only once a year, on the Day of Atonement, they assembled in the synagogue to listen to the cantor pray for them and hear him read from the Torah.

On the night before Yom Kippur, the sexton came to the synagogue in order to make it ready for the Holy Day. He suddenly saw the little doors of the Holy Ark open. He watched in silent wonder as scores of alphabet letters flew out from the inner darkness of the Ark, like swarms of angry bees tossed out by a concealed hand. The letters arranged themselves in lines and rows. Like an unfurled fiery scroll, they flew out through the open window and disappeared in the dark blue sky of the night.

"The Torah has abandoned us!" the sexton cried with terror in his voice.

"No, it is you who have abandoned the Torah," a voice from the Ark answered.

On that Yom Kippur day when the scrolls were taken from the Ark and unrolled before the assembled congregation, the worshippers were horrified to see the white parchment blank, as

38

though nothing had ever been written upon it.

On that same day a miracle happened in the synagogue of the oppressed Jewish community. When the Jews took out their blank scroll and unrolled it, they were amazed to see that the white sheets were covered with letters and lines. Every letter was in its place. Not one was missing. The blind reader suddenly regained his sight and joyfully read the Torah to the whole congregation.

Sometime after that Jews from the first community visited the second community. They told their more fortunate brothers how hard life was under the rule of the tyrant. They also told them about the miracle that happened in their congregation. It was then that the Jews who lived in the second community realized where the letters of their Torah had disappeared.

They brought their persecuted brothers to their community and established a great and famous college that produced many noted and distinguished scholars. And the city became known to all Jews throughout the world as "The Second Jerusalem."

To the King's Blacksmith

NEAR a thick spreading oak tree at the side of a broad highway leading to a small Jewish town in Lithuania, stood an old, old stone smithy. No one knew how long this smithy had been standing there—not even the old Jewish blacksmith who now lived in it. He knew only that in this very shop where he worked, his father, his father's father before him and even his great, great grandfather, all had lived and worked there. This smithy was famous throughout the entire region both in Jewish and non-Jewish settlements, because of its curious name. It was called "By the Sign of the King's Blacksmith."

It was said that long, long ago, in the far distant past, a Jewish blacksmith had worked there. He was a very simple man who did not even know how to read. He was, however, a very pious and a very honest man. He did not worship in the usual manner. Instead, he had his own little prayer which he repeated every morning when he lighted the fire in the pit. He prayed, "Lord of the Universe, make it so that my labors will be a help to man and not to harm him. Let them be for good and not for evil."

And so the blacksmith lived quietly, going about his work shoeing the hooves of the peasants' horses, repairing their ploughs and the wheels of their wagons.

One day, two knights on horseback rode up to his shop and asked the blacksmith to put new shoes on the hooves of their horses. These knights were on a secret mission for the king. They were on their way to punish severely the count who owned this territory. The count had been falsely accused by enemies of plotting against the king.

The knights left the blacksmith's shop as soon as their horses were shod. They rode through a dense forest. When they were deep in the woods their horses suddenly came to a halt and would go no further. Their new shoes seemed wedged into the ground and their feet were like lead. The stirrups became so tight about the legs of the knights that they could not dismount. They remained in one position, unable to move.

41

In the meantime, good friends had been able to prove to the king that the count was innocent. As soon as the king convinced himself that the accusations were false, he dispatched two other knights with orders to stop the first two knights from punishing the count. When these two messengers rode into the forest and found the knights still there, they asked in surprise why they were waiting.

"It is because of the Jew," they answered. "He bewitched the shoes he put on the hooves of our horses."

"If he did that," said the knights who had just arrived, "he served a just cause. The count is innocent and the king has sent us to cancel his order to punish him."

The four knights then proceeded to the castle of the count. When they told him the story about the blacksmith and the horseshoes he had bewitched, the count saddled his horse and went to see the Jewish blacksmith.

"Were you the one who put new shoes on the hooves of the horses belonging to two of the king's knights riding past here?" asked the count.

"Yes, my Lord," replied the blacksmith.

"Did you know where the knights were going?" again asked the count.

"No, my Lord," answered the smith. "I did not."

The count then told the blacksmith about the knights and what had happened. The blacksmith listened and became very thoughtful. Finally he remarked very quietly, "Now I know that God hears my prayer."

Some time after that the king died and the count was chosen as his successor. The new king called the blacksmith to him and said, "As of to-day, I appoint you my personal blacksmith.

Whenever I shall send my knights on a mission you shall put new shoes on the hooves of their horses."

And so it was. Each time the king sent a knight with an order and the knight did not arrive at the specified place, the king would know that his command was unjust and he recalled it. It was at that time that the old smithy was named "By the Sign of the King's Blacksmith."

The Fiddler and the Count

A LONG, long time ago, hundreds of years ago, a Polish count ordered all Jews to leave his town. He gave them three days time to settle all their affairs.

The order came during an exceptionally cold and bitter winter. It was so cold that the black crows, nesting in the tall pines that surrounded the church, froze to death. The little town lay buried under the deep snow. If it were not for the wisps of blue smoke rising from the little chimneys towards the sky, one might have thought that the town had vanished.

When the Jews learned of the cruel command, they declared a day of fasting. Everyone assembled in the synagogue and prayed that God might hear them and help them. Only one man remained calm. His name was Moishe Motye, the fiddler. He did not go to the synagogue. He remained in his little house behind the public bath and played mournful tunes on his fiddle. He played as he usually played, with his eyes shut.

That same day the count left his palace and went on a hunting trip in the forest. In the evening, when the sun began to set, he was surrounded by a huge pack of hungry wolves with fiery eyes. The count quickly climbed a tall tree. The wolves encircled the tree and sat down, with their heads turned upwards towards the Count. They waited for him to either come down or fall down.

The night air got colder and colder. The count felt icy fingers of frost gripping his body and the blood chill in his veins. He became drowsy and was about to fall asleep when it seemed to him that he heard the plaintive sounds of a violin in the distance. The melancholy tune came nearer and nearer, and presently Moishe Motye appeared between the trees, playing his fiddle. The wolves pricked up their ears, turned their heads towards Moishe Motye and began to howl. They howled and wailed for a long time. Finally they got up and disappeared in the wilds of the woods.

The count climbed down from the tree, and without even a glance at Moishe Motye, turned and left. He went home to his castle.

The following morning, the count, accompanied by his armed soldiers, arrived in town. They rounded up all the Jews and brought them into the courtyard of the synagogue. The count then ordered them to leave town at once.

Suddenly the door of the synagogue opened and framed in the doorway stood Moishe Motye playing his fiddle.

"Are you here again, you cursed musician?" angrily shouted the count. "Do you think I am a wolf and you can drive me into the forest by the witchery of your fiddle?"

"If the heart within you is not a human heart," Moishe Motye said quietly, "I shall then play for you as though you were a wolf."

No sooner did Moishe Motye utter these words than the count jumped off his horse, crouched on all fours, and raising his head towards the sky, started to howl like a wolf. Moishe Motye played and played until the count, still howling, left the town and disappeared from sight in the forest.

Servants found the count some time later. He was lying under a tree grovelling in the snow. They had to tie him and take him to the capitol city where he was kept behind iron bars. The count's brother came to live in the palace and took his place. He cancelled the inhuman directive which the count had made against the Jews.

No one ever saw Moishe Motye after that. His little house remained unoccupied. Old and pious Jews in town said that Moishe Motye surely was more than an ordinary fiddler. They said he must have been one of the thirty-six unknown Saints.

The Tree of a Martyr

ONCE upon a time, a very long time ago, there was a young count who lived near **Vilna**. He came from a very old aristocratic and wealthy family. The young count interested himself in the Jews of his region. When he learned about their laws and their customs, he converted to Judaism and became a very pious Jew.

In vain did his family plead with him and beg him to return to his former way of life. The Church threatened him with the most severe punishment, but he remained steadfast in his new found faith.

At that time it was considered a crime to convert to Judaism. The count was arrested and sentenced to be burned at the stake in the public square of Vilno.

The execution took place, and that night the Jews came and gathered up his ashes. They buried them in the Jewish cemetery.

But behold the wonder! A short time after the ashes were buried, a most extraordinary tree grew on the grave of the convert. From one root sprouted four branches. These branches, however, did not rise upward towards the sky. They lay flat across the grave like arms and legs outstretched, giving the impression of one lying prostrate in prayer before God.

The Jews sanctified the grave of this convert. People from both near and far came to pay homage to his memory and to pray for his soul.

Many years later, another count with his retinue of followers rode past the Jewish cemetery where the ashes of the holy convert were buried. This count was a distant relative of the holy convert, and out of curiosity went into the cemetery to see the unusual tree.

"This is a sign of humility," said the count as he gazed at the figure of supplication. He ordered his attendants to cut off the four branches and take them to the old ancestral home.

The following morning when the count awoke and looked out from his palace window, he was amazed to see that the four branches had taken root and were standing upright. They looked fresh and green as if they had been growing there for a long time. Four other branches grew on the grave of the martyr. They lay flat across the grave in the same position as the original branches.

More years passed. Then the rebellion of the Poles against the Russians took place. Poland had been oppressed by Russia for a long time and finally the Polish people rebelled against the Russian rule. The count was captured and brought back to his own castle as a prisoner.

They hanged the count at night by the light of torches. They hanged him from one of the four trees that had been brought from the convert's grave. No one had noticed that one of its branches had lifted itself and supported the count's feet, so that he remained alive. As soon as the Russians left, the tree bent slowly downward until it lay flat on the ground.

At dawn, with the first rays of the morning sun, the count regained consciousness. He found himself lying on the soft grass and saw that the four branches were lying stretched on the ground exactly as they had been on the martyr's grave. "Your faith, my dear distant cousin, has saved my life," the count said quietly to himself. He picked himself up from the ground and disappeared in the neighboring forest.

No one ever saw him after that. But rumor among the Jews in that area is very strong that hidden in some House of Worship in some little Jewish town, the count is studying the Torah the same way as his saintly relative did long, long ago.

The Miracle of the Chanukah Candles

THERE was once a wealthy forest land dealer who lived in a Jewish town in Lithuania. In spite of his wealth, this merchant was a very pious man. He had a kind heart and was very generous to all the needy.

The holiday of Chanukah was of special significance to him and he observed the lighting of the Chanukah candles most de-

votedly. He had to travel about a great deal because of his business and was on the road constantly. During the week of Chanukah he always carried a package of small wax candles with him
so that no matter where he happened to be, whether on the road
or at an inn, he was able to light the little candles and thank
God for the miracle that had happened to the Jews during the
time of the Hasmoneans.

One Chanukah, the day the seventh candle was to be lighted,
the merchant went to see a nobleman who lived in a castle which
was situated deep in the forest among the pine woods. He had a
business matter to discuss and carried a large sum of money with
him.

The forest merchant employed a coachman who drove him
regularly. The coachman was a local peasant who was very
familiar with every path and every road in the immense forest.
When the coachman learned that the merchant was carrying
a lot of money, he decided to lead the merchant astray in the
dense woods. He planned to leave him there for the night, and
hoped that the wolves would get him. He would then be able to
take the money.

And the peasant carried out his plan. Instead of driving directly to the nobleman's castle, he drove around for hours
through the snow covered forest. When night fell and it grew
very dark, he left the merchant alone in the heart of the desolate
forest and went away. The peasant climbed a tree and sat there,
waiting for the passing of the night.

When the merchant realized that he had been left alone and
deserted in the wilds of the forest, he found a spot that was
sheltered by a clump of little fir trees. Putting his fate into the
hands of God, he decided to remain there through the night.

He took out the package of little candles, and brushing the snow from one of the green twigs of a tree, he secured seven little candles to it. He said his evening prayers and thanked God for the great miracle of Chanukah.

Suddenly he became aware of the fiery, burning eyes of hungry wolves looking at him from between the trunks of the trees. They had encircled his little spot and were edging closer and closer towards him. At that moment the seven little candles burst into a huge torchlike flame. The glistening snow on the fir tree reflected the fire with a million brilliant sparks and it looked as if the entire tree were ablaze.

The fire frightened the wolves and they remained standing at a distance. And so the seven little wax candles burned on throughout that long winter night and did not blow out.

Dawn finally came and the wolves left. The timber merchant seated himself in his carriage and allowed the horse to lead him out of the forest. The horse brought him safely to the nobleman's castle.

Several days later the evil coachman was found lying under a tall pine tree. He had frozen to death while sitting in the tree and his body had fallen to the ground.

A Bird's Nest

NOT too far from a small Jewish town in Lithuania lived a farmer with his wife and their little boy. This little boy was a very mean child who had no love nor pity for any of God's creatures. One day he climbed on the roof of his father's house and destroyed a bird's nest where three little swallows were sitting under their mother's wing. The little swallows fell to the ground when the nest was destroyed.

At dawn, at the start of a new day, all creatures raise their voices in song to their Creator. God listened to the chorus of the world that morning and missed the tiny voices of the three little swallows. Then the mother came and charged the little boy with breaking the commandment in the Torah that forbids anyone to take little birds away from under a mother's wing.

Many years passed. The little boy grew up and became a man. He married and had three beautiful little boys of his own. The children were very bright, but none of them was able to talk. They were all mute.

When the oldest son was almost thirteen and about to celebrate his Bar Mitzvah, the father had a strange dream. He dreamed that an old man stood before him and said, "If you wish to hear your children talk, get up at once and go into the woods. You will see an oak that has been felled to the ground. Under this tree you will find three little birds. Take these little birds home with you and keep them until I come again."

The father woke up. He dressed quickly, took his cane and left the house. It was a frosty winter night and a violent storm raged across the fields. The air was so cold that the breath froze on the lips and the night was so dark that it was impossible to see three paces ahead.

As soon as the father reached the woods he noticed a little light among the branches of the trees. The light bobbed before him on the snow. He followed it until he came to a branch of an oak which had been hewn down. He shoveled the deep snow away with his hands and found three half frozen little birds. The father picked these little birds up very carefully and put them on his chest under his clothes to keep them warm. And he brought them home with him.

The little birds soon revived and flew about the house all winter long. However, they were mute, as mute as his own children. They never uttered even as much as a tweet.

At last the long winter was over and spring came, bringing with it the beautiful Passover holiday.

It was the first Seder night. The entire family sat at the table. A beautiful white cloth covered the table and a cup filled with wine was set at the side of each plate. In the center stood a silver goblet filled with wine for the Prophet Elijah.

At the proper moment the door opened and an old man with a white beard entered. He picked up the silver goblet, blessed the wine and allowed each child to sip from it. The little birds also flew to the goblet and dipped their beaks in the wine. Suddenly the boys began to talk and the birds began to sing. Then, flying in a circle above the old man's head, the little birds disappeared with him through the open door into the blue of the spring night.

Meyer Baer

A GYPSY with a big brown bear once came to a small Jewish town in Lithuania. An iron ring with a very heavy chain hung from the bear's nose. Every afternoon the gypsy brought the bear to the market place. The gypsy beat on his drum and made the bear dance by cracking a whip.

One Friday afternoon the bear refused to dance because he was hungry. The gypsy was whipping the bear savagely when Reb Meyer, the richest business man in town, happened to pass by. Reb Meyer was noted for his piety and kindness. Seeing the gypsy whip the bear, Reb Meyer asked, "Why do you beat this poor hungry animal?"

"If you don't like the way I treat him," said the gypsy, "Buy the bear from me and you can feed him with milk and honey."

"How much do you want for him?" inquired Reb Meyer.

Feeling sure that the Jew did not mean to buy the bear, the gypsy answered, "Twenty gold coins."

"That's a deal," said Reb Meyer. He paid the gypsy the price he had asked and took the bear along with him.

"I have brought a guest home with me for the Sabbath," Reb Meyer told his astonished family when they saw him with the bear. He sat the bear down in a corner of the courtyard and went to the synagogue. When he returned he took the bear into the house. Reb Meyer made Kiddush and washed his hands. He recited the blessing over the Hallah, and after cutting it, he gave the first piece to his guest, the bear.

All that Sabbath day the bear sat in Reb Meyer's house. Soon after the day was done Reb Meyer led the bear into the woods. He removed the chains from the bear and said, "Go in peace, Friend Baer, and do no harm to good men."

Shortly after that Reb Meyer went on a business trip with his partner. Their way led through a dense forest and they got lost. Friday afternoon Reb Meyer decided to go no further. He wished to remain where he was and rest for the Sabbath. His partner, however, wished to keep going. They divided the money and whatever food they had. The partner took the horse and buggy and went on his way, leaving Reb Meyer alone in the forest.

At sundown, as he stood saying his evening prayers, Reb Meyer felt a heavy paw on his shoulder. He turned his head and saw a big brown bear at his side. The bear was looking at him, and his eyes were filled with human kindness. Reb Meyer immediately recognized this bear as the one he had set free.

"Good Sabbath to you," Reb Meyer greeted the bear.

"Boo, boo, boo," softly growled the bear in reply. The bear picked up Reb Meyer's bag and carried it to his cave. All that Sabbath day Reb Meyer was the guest of the bear. In the evening, right after Havdallah, the bear once again picked up Reb Meyer's bag and started to lead him out of the forest.

They reached the edge of the woods at dawn. Reb Meyer noticed a band of robbers lying under a tree, and tied to that tree was his partner. Before the bandits had a chance to get up from the ground, the bear attacked and killed them. Reb Meyer untied his partner and both joyfully returned to their homes.

Since that time Reb Meyer was called "Meyer Baer." And the name "Meyer-Baer" has remained in the family ever since.

Rabbi Soos

THIS was the only horse in the world that was called with the title "Rabbi." How he earned this title is quite a story and worth telling.

Far away, in one of the lesser known Jewish little towns there once lived a coachman by the name of Rachmiel, the Reciter of Psalms. Rachmiel was an ordinary God-fearing Jew with broad shoulders and a heavy red beard. He was no scholar, but he knew all the psalms by heart. Their tune was ever in his heart, and the words were on his lips. He recited and sang them continuously at home or on the road; while greasing the wheels of his coach or hitching his horse.

One day Rachmiel's horse died and he was too poor to buy another. His entire fortune consisted of five Imperial dollars which he did not want to touch. He did not, however, despair. His faith in the Almighty was boundless and he knew that somehow God would help him. "Don't you worry," he comforted his wife, "God will help."

"Yes, yes," she once answered bitterly when there was no more money to buy food for the children, "I know that God, will help eventually, but who will help us in the meantime?"

Rachmiel was disturbed and deeply hurt by his wife's words. He took the precious five gold pieces and his whip and walked to the neighboring town where a sale of horses was being held. "Perhaps God will help me and I will be able to find a bargain," thought Rachmiel.

When Rachmiel reached the town, the market place was filled with peasants and horse traders. As he walked among them he noticed a tall slender Jew standing apart from the others. He seemed lost in thought. His eyes were raised towards the heavens and his hand rested on the halter of a fine brown horse standing beside him. Rachmiel approached the Jew and casually asked whether he wanted to sell the horse.

"Yes," was the Jew's curt reply.

"And what might the price be for such a horse?" inquired Rachmiel.

"This horse is worth thirty pieces of gold, but I will sell him to you for twenty," offered the Jew.

"It is a bargain, indeed," said Rachmiel sadly, "but not for me."

"Why not?" questioned the Jew.

"Because all I have is five gold pieces," answered Rachmiel.

"That does not matter," the strange Jew said. "Give me the five gold pieces and take the horse. You will return the rest when God will help you. But there is one thing that you must remember. This horse is accustomed to observe the Sabbath. He stops work on Friday, one hour before candle lighting time and will make no move until after the Sabbath."

"He shall be well taken care of," promised Rachmiel. He thanked the Jew and took the horse back home with him.

"This was none other than the Prophet Elijah," thought Rachmiel. But he kept this thought to himself and said nothing about it to anyone. Rachmiel again had a horse and once again drove passengers to and from the big city.

All would have gone well if it were not for the shopkeepers. They went to the city every Thursday to buy merchandise to market on Sunday. They were in the habit of leaving late on Thursday and were therefore barely able to complete their business and return home an hour before sundown on Friday.

One time Rachmiel and his passengers were caught in a sudden thunderstorm on their return trip from the city. They were half way home when the road turned into a quagmire of mud. They did not stop, however. They plodded on with great difficulty. When they came to within a half mile from town, the horse stopped and refused to go any further. The passengers were very angry and swore at the horse, but the horse stood motionless. The shopkeepers had to trudge the half mile to town through the mud and the slush carrying their wares with them.

"It is your own fault," shouted Rachmiel after the merchants. "You should take a lesson from this pious animal and learn how to observe the Sabbath."

It was at that time that the horse was named "Rabbi Soos," or "Rabbi Horse."

Rachmiel discovered yet another remarkable characteristic in his horse. It was evident that the horse possessed a sixth sense. He seemed to know in advance whether or not they would arrive in time, when there would be a rainstorm in the summer or a snowstorm in the winter. All Rachmiel had to do was to ask, "Rabbi Soos, will we be back before it is time to light the candles, or not?" The horse would raise his head and sniff the air. If he pricked up his ears it would mean, "Yes." If he lowered his head and dropped his ears it meant, "No."

Now, there were two thieves in town and they decided to make Rachmiel's horse a partner in their crimes. One dark and gloomy night they stole Rabbi Soos from his stall and disappeared with him. In the morning when the news of the horse's disappearance spread about the town, the storekeepers laughed at Rachmiel and taunted him saying, "So your saint, Rabbi Soos, allowed himself to be led away without uttering a sound!"

"Don't you worry," Rachmiel calmly replied. "He will be back." And so he was.

The thieves had taken Rabbi Soos to a nearby town. They harnessed him to a wagon and prepared to carry out an old scheme of theirs. They planned to rob the rich Polish squire who lived in an isolated little hunting lodge in the forest. He lived with just two servants and four hunters.

It so happened that the squire together with the hunters and their dogs left very early that Friday morning to shoot wild ducks. The robbers came and overpowered the servants. They tied them up and took an iron safe containing a great deal of gold. They placed the safe on the wagon with Rabbi Soos harnessed to it and covered it with hay. They then started on their way to an inn where they were well known, traveling on roads that were seldom used.

In the meantime the sun began to set and the hour before candle lighting time arrived. Rabbi Soos stopped and stood still. The thieves beat him, pulled at the halter and pushed the wagon, but the horse refused to budge. He dug both his forelegs into the ground, flattened his ears and stood as if he were glued to the ground.

At that moment the squire and the four hunters appeared from the forest. "This is the first time I have ever seen such a stubborn horse," said the squire, and they all remained to watch the spectacle.

"Punch him in the snoot," advised one of the hunters.

One of the thieves came up to the horse and punched him in the nose. Rabbi Soos instantly stood up on his hind legs, raised his forelegs and with one heave, turned the wagon over. The hay which had been piled on top of the wagon fell off and the squire recognized his iron safe containing the gold.

A very strange procession marched into the town market place on Sunday morning. Leading the procession was Rabbi Soos. He walked slowly and deliberately, without a halter, his head lowered. Behind him marched the four hunters carrying the two thieves who had been bound tightly. The squire, riding on his horse, brought up the rear, followed by two wagons loaded with sacks of the very finest oats. When Rabbi Soos reached Rachmiel's house, he went directly into his stall.

"Is this your horse?" the squire asked Rachmiel who had come out of his little house.

"Yes, sire."

"I have heard that he is a very pious horse who observes your Sabbath."

"Yes, sire. So is his custom here."

"Because of his custom, he has done me a great service." Pointing his finger at the two wagons heavily loaded with oats, the squire continued, "This is his reward. When he will need more you can always come to me."

After that, the townspeople looked at Rachmiel's horse with new respect and admiration. The merchants made special efforts to leave early and always arrived back home one hour before it was time to light the Sabbath candles.

The Story About a Grandma and a Grandpa

ONCE upon a time in a little house with a garden, there lived a grandmother and a grandfather. They had a cat, a goat, two chickens and a rooster. The old folks were very pious and loved their animals dearly. Every morning after prayers, as they sat down to eat breakfast, the grandfather would remark, "Sarah, my dear wife, you know that our Jewish law tells us that animals must be fed before we eat."

And the grandmother always answered, "You are right my husband." She then proceeded to feed the animals. She brought out a big pail of potato peelings with pieces of bread and vegetables for the goat and a small bowl of milk for the cat. For the fowl, she filled her apron with kernels of corn and scattered them over the courtyard.

And their animals were just as good and kind as were the old folks. The goat never stole anything from strange gardens and the chickens never laid eggs in hidden places. They had two little baskets in the kitchen where they sat to lay their eggs. After they had laid the eggs they came to the grandmother and cackled, "Ka, ka, ka," meaning, "Mistress, we have already laid the eggs."

The rooster took his place at the grandfather's bed every morning at dawn as soon as the blue of the sky tinted the little window. He crowed and crowed until the grandfather got up, dressed and went to say his prayers. The cat always sat near the board on which the grandmother salted her kosher meat. She watched that her kittens should not, God forbid, touch the meat. If one of the kittens came a little too close to the meat, the mother cat would slap it with her paw.

One time the grandmother brought home some meat that she had bought from a new butcher. She soaked and salted the meat as usual, and cut off a piece for the cat. But the cat refused to touch it. She sniffed it, shook her paw, hunched her back and spat at it.

The grandmother could not understand the cat's strange behavior, and when the grandfather returned from the synagogue she told him about it. "Something must be wrong with the cat," she said. "She seems well enough, but she will not touch the meat." The following day another strange thing happened. The cat did not watch the meat on the board. She allowed her kittens to do whatever they pleased. The grandmother was very upset. "Our cat has never done such a thing," she complained to the grandfather. On the third morning the rooster failed to wake up the grandfather and he was late for prayers.

"Do you know, my dear wife, Sarah," said the grandfather, "I too, am beginning to think that something is not right in our home."

However, it was only when the chickens hid themselves some-place in the attic to lay their eggs and the goat came home with a head of cabbage which she had stolen from a neighbor's gar-den, that the grandmother became frightened and ran crying bitterly to the grandfather. "Something is very, very wrong here in our home," she sobbed. "The whole world seems topsy turvy. I feel that the whole trouble started with the meat. I am afraid that the meat is not kosher."

The grandfather then decided to tell the rabbi about their problems. They dressed in their good clothes which they wore only on holidays and the Sabbath and went to see the rabbi.

The rabbi listened very attentively to their story. After much thought, he finally said, "We shall see."

As soon as the grandmother and grandfather left, the rabbi called a meeting of the council members. He told them the story he had heard from the old folks and instructed them to watch the butcher very closely.

That night the watchman caught the butcher smuggling into town a non-kosher ox from some other village. The butcher was driven from town at once. Another butcher, a pious and honest man was brought in.

With the arrival of the good butcher everything returned to normal in the little house where the grandmother and grandfather lived. The cat ate the meat, the chickens once again laid their eggs in their little baskets, the rooster started to wake the grandfather in time to go to the synagogue and the goat nodded piously with her little beard. She ate from the pail and never again stole anything from strange gardens. Since that time, grandmother always gave the cat a larger portion of meat, saying to the grandfather, "Who knows? If it were not for the animals the whole world might have been destroyed."

This complete story was later carefully noted in the congregation's Book of Records so that their children and their children's children might read about it. And it was from this Book of Records that I copied this story.

The Tailor and the Sprite

LONG ago, in ancient times, a tailor by the name of Nohte lived in a little Jewish town in Lithuania. He was a very average individual; short, slight of build, with a beard that was sparse and grey. His eyes were bright and intelligent and always seemed to smile from under his high forehead. He was known as the greatest wit in town and from time to time he loved to play practical jokes.

Every Sunday morning, Nohte packed his shears and his iron, his needles and thread into a big sack and toured the villages making new clothes or mending the old for the villagers. The peasants paid him in different ways. Some paid with a bag of dried peas, lentils or beans; some, with a live rooster or goose; and some, with money. Thursday morning he was on the road again, homeward bound, his big sack loaded with enough supplies to last his family for a week.

Nohte lived quietly and without excitement until the incident with the sprite who laughed at the townspeople.

It was a warm Sabbath evening in the summer. While taking a leisurely stroll, a group of boys came upon the ruins of an old castle not too far out of town. One wall and a high round tower was all that remained of this castle. At the base of the tower there was a big opening leading to a deep, deep cellar.

The night was calm, and the moon, like a big bright lantern, hung high above the tower. The boys decided to look down into the opening at the base of the tower. Fearing that evil spirits might be lurking in the dark cellar, the boys, being devout Jews took all necessary precautions to ward them off. First, they gathered in their right hands all four tzitziz of the ritual undershirts they were wearing. Then they put their heads into the hole and shouted as with one voice, "HEAR, O ISRAEL!"

Immediately they heard a voice laughing. It came from the innermost depth of the cellar and sounded very much like the hoarse bass voice of the old cantor. The boys knew at once that a *letz,* (a sprite) was hiding in the cellar of the ruined castle and they ran back to town, broadcasting the news.

Old people sitting on the porches of their homes questioned

the boys at length. Finally they announced with a sigh, "There will be trouble." They did not have long to wait. Trouble did come.

On the morning of the following Thursday the butcher went to the village, as usual, to buy a couple of calves and a cow so that the Jews would have meat for the Sabbath. The road stretched along the edge of a pine forest. As he walked along he noticed a big, fat calf lying before him, all tied up.

"Ho, ho," exclaimed the butcher happily, "such a bargain I did not expect." Not wasting any time on thought, he put the calf on his shoulders and started back to town. Strangely enough, the calf grew bigger and bigger until it became as big and heavy as an ox. In vain did the butcher try to free himself from his burden. The calf sat firmly on his shoulders, as though it had grown onto them. At last the calf released the butcher and flew like a bird to the top of a tree. It crowed twice like a rooster and disappeared, laughing wildly.

The butcher reached town half dead with fright and went directly to bed. That Sabbath there was no meat for the Jews.

"This is only the beginning," warned the old folks. "This *letz* is a bad one, it seems."

They were right again. That very night the *letz* played another trick. This time, the victim was none other than the rabbi of the town.

The hour was late. As he so often did, the rabbi had remained alone in the darkened House of Prayer. He was absorbed in a book, reading by the light of a small candle. From the other end of the synagogue, from the women's gallery, there suddenly appeared a long red tongue, like a snake. A little mound of

71

strong tobacco was on its tip, and before the rabbi knew it, the tongue with the tobacco on its tip was right under his nose. It disappeared immediately, but the rabbi saw it. For three days the rabbi sneezed, had a running nose and was unable to catch his breath.

After this episode, the rabbi met with the important men of the town and discussed means of getting rid of the *letz*. All night they sat thinking and exchanging ideas, but came to no conclusion. Towards dawn, Moishe the shoemaker came in and said that he had a solution.

Moishe's grandfather was a very learned man and knew the characteristics of all the spirits. He once told him that there was only one sure way to drive a *letz* from a town. Someone must be found who could trick the *letz*. If that were possible, the *letz* would be so ashamed and embarrassed that he would have to leave town.

The rabbi and the others liked Moishe's suggestion. But who could outsmart the *letz?* After much thought they all agreed that Nohte was the man who could do it.

All that week the townspeople waited for Nohte to return from the villages. At last it was Thursday afternoon and they saw him coming with the sack on his back and a big rooster under his arm.

The rabbi, accompanied by the town's most eminent men, went forth to greet Nohte and welcome him back home. Very slowly and deliberately, Nohte took the sack from his shoulders and put the rooster down on the ground. He tugged at his sparse little beard for some time, all the while looking at the rabbi and the men with clever eyes. Finally, pointing a finger at himself, he asked, "Do you know who I am?"

"Nohte," was the reply.

"And what day is this?"

"Thursday."

"And on what day will the Ninth of Ab be this year?"

"On a Sunday."

"Well," said Nohte, "in that case I see you are not clowning. Would you be good enough to tell me what I did to deserve such honor?"

"Nohte," the rabbi said, "we have come to beg you in the name of the entire congregation, to do something to drive the *letz* from our town."

"Oh, is that why you came?" exclaimed Nohte still tugging at his little beard and staring at them. "I thought you had mistaken me for the Prophet Elijah."

"Please, Nohte, don't make fun of us," begged the men. "The problem is a very serious one."

"All right, all right. We shall see," promised Nohte. He heaved the sack on his shoulders, and taking the rooster under his arm, went home.

Nohte did not appear in the street all that Thursday. No one saw him all day Friday, either. In the evening he came to the synagogue as usual, but spoke to no one. He kept tugging at his beard and smiling to himself.

"Nohte has a trick up his sleeve," the Jews told each other quietly. And they waited.

Saturday evening, after Havdalah, Nohte sauntered casually towards the abandoned castle. Hands clasped behind his back and chanting a hymn in his nasal tone, he approached the old tower. Nohte stationed himself before the hole and called, "Shalom Aleichem, *Letz.*"

"Aleichem Shalom, Nohte," a voice from the cellar replied.

"I come to make a deal with you," continued Nohte.

"Let's hear," the bass voice invited.

"I'll give you three days time. If within that time you can trick me, then I, Nohte, will leave town. If, however, I trick you within that time, then you must leave."

"I agree!" The voice consented and then burst into laughter, "Ha, ha, ha . . ."

Sunday morning, as soon as the sun rose, Nohte was on the road again. He carried with him his sack with his shears, press iron and his needles and threads. He walked along singing one of the cantor's new tunes while plucking his beard and gazing at the sky. His foot tripped on something in the road and looking down, he saw a fur jacket. The jacket was made of fine black sheepskins, such as only the rich Polish gentry wore.

Nohte picked up the coat, and shaking it free of the dust, said out loud, "Hm, hm, hm. What an exceptionally fine garment this is. This jacket is probably worth a hundred or more. Let's see how it is made."

Nohte sat down on a rock. He took a big needle and a long thread from his pocket and quickly started to sew the fur together. First he sewed up the bottom, then the sleeves, and the collar last. When he finished sewing, the coat looked like a bag. "And now," said Nohte, "I better beat the dust out." He broke off a heavy twig from the branch of a tree and began beating the fur.

"Nohte," the fur coat begged, "rip out the stitches and let me out of here. I swear to you, I will leave town."

"Shalom Aleichem," Nohte said in feigned surprise. "It never occurred to me that you were the fur jacket. All good things come unexpectedly. Don't you think so, *Letz?*"

"Have pity," cried the voice. "Rip the stitches. I beg of you."

"You are quite right. But you will have to wait a bit. You know that I am a poor tailor and the peasants are expecting me in the village. Get back to your cellar, meanwhile, and wait there for me until Saturday night. Then, with God's help, I'll come and rip the stitches out." With that, he kicked the baloon-like fur with his boot and added, "Now get going. Let me see how you can run on your sleeves."

Nohte stood watching the fur jacket for a long time as it ran on its two sleeves towards the town. "There will be a gay time in town tonight," said Nohte to himself.

The first to see the fur coat running were the boys who had heard the *letz* laughing in the cellar. They started after the fur with sticks and stones, shouting, "Hooray, the *letz* is on the run!"

Immediately, everyone ran out of their houses; the shoemaker with a skin of leather in his hand, the tailor with his metal measuring stick, the blacksmith with his hammer and the house-wives with their brooms. Blows from every direction rained on the fur jacket. Even the public goat and the black dog that be-longed to the Gentile who did the Sabbath chores joined in the free-for-all. Bucking the coat with the horns and tearing at the fur, they followed it to the old tower where it disappeared into the hole.

Thursday afternoon, as usual, Nohte returned home. The sack on his shoulder was heavily loaded and under his arm he car-ried a goose. By this time, everyone in town knew that Nohte had sewn the *letz* into the fur. Nohte, however, had nothing to say. He answered all questions with a tug at his beard and "This is a tailor's secret."

The end of the story was that the next Sunday morning, Nohte did not, as had been his custom, leave for the ·villages. Instead, he sat on the porch of his home blissfully smoking his pipe. It is the belief of the townspeople that the *letz* paid Nohte a handsome ransom for liberating him from the fur. Some say that the *letz* gave Nohte a pot full of gold which he had found buried in the cellar. Others say that the *letz* brings him a bag of money every Saturday night. Nohte himself never revealed which one of these theories is true. Since that time, however, not one *letz* ever again appeared in this town.

The Miller's Helper

LITTLE Isaac was an orphan. His mother had died at his birth and his father died a year later. He was completely alone. There was no one in his family to care for him and he became the ward of the community. The teacher in the public classroom agreed to take the child and the community paid for his care.

Years passed and Isaac grew tall and strong. When he was twelve, he looked like an eighteen year old. He was a fine boy, but a very, very poor scholar. He tried hard and studied diligently, but whatever he learned during the day he forgot at night. Finally, when he reached his thirteenth birthday his teacher said, "My poor child, I know it is not your fault. You have studied faithfully and well, but you are handicapped by a closed mind. You are well and strong. Go out into the world and earn your bread honestly by working with your hands."

Isaac's heart was heavy and his eyes filled with tears as he took leave from his teacher. He left his little town and hired himself out as a handyman to a Jewish miller who owned a windmill. All day long he dragged sacks of corn uphill and sacks of flour downhill. At night, after supper, he went to his little room, and before going to bed he repeated his own special prayer, "Lord of the Universe, I beg of you, open my mind and clear my thoughts so that I may be able to study your Torah, for that is my only wish."

One day on his way to work in the windmill Isaac saw two runaway horses heading directly towards the edge of a cliff, carrying with them a wagonful of people. Desperate cries for help came from the women and children in the wagon. Isaac ran towards the horses and at the risk of his own life held them back until everyone in the wagon was safely out. Only then did he let go and the horses together with the wagon plunged down the cliff.

That night when he opened the door of his little room, he was greeted by a most amazing sight. The little room was flooded with a glorious light, and sitting at the table was a stately old man reading from a book.

"Don't be frightened," the old man said. "Your heroism this morning has been well marked. Your prayer has been heard and I have been sent to study the Torah with you. But this you must remember: No one must know about this until the proper time."

And the old man came to study with Isaac every night until Isaac became a very learned man and so wise that he knew the answers to all the secrets of the earth.

A famous rabbi from a large Jewish community once drove past the windmill. It was a dark and stormy evening. The hour was growing late, and the rabbi decided to spend the night at the miller's house. Late that night the rabbi went for a walk, and passing the door of Isaac's little room, he suddenly saw the extraordinary light shining through its cracks. The rabbi looked into the room through one of the cracks and saw Isaac and the old man bent over a book. The rabbi knew at once that Isaac was no ordinary laborer, but a great scholar. However, he made no mention to anyone of what he had seen. He returned to his home town the following day.

The rabbi died not too long after that. When the elders of the congregation read his will they learned that the rabbi wished them to appoint the handyman from the windmill to succeed him. They delegated several of their outstanding members to go to the windmill and bring Isaac back with them to the city. When Isaac came, the elders of the community honored their old rabbi's request and appointed Isaac as their rabbi.

Isaac became famous as the most learned man of his time, and his word was law unto all Jews.

A Journey through the Sabbath

"GET Chestnut out of the stable
and take him into the meadow," said Eli's father. "Let him, too,
enjoy the delights of the Sabbath. He has worked hard all week."

Eli did not have to be coaxed to get Chestnut. Chestnut was
the name of their brown horse and was considered as one of the
family, for without him there would be no bread to eat. Eli ran
to the stable as soon as the family finished the Sabbath noon
meal and had offered their thanks to God.

Eli's father was a teamster who carted merchandise and passengers between the little Jewish town and its neighboring big city. Eli had just passed his thirteenth birthday and was still a pupil at the *cheder*. The horse was his very best friend. They loved each other and understood one another by the wink of an eye. The family always said that Eli and the horse had their own secret sign language in which they talked to each other.

It was Eli's privilege to lead the horse into the field every Saturday afternoon during the summer months. Other horses whose owners were Jews were also taken into the field. They were at pasture all day on the Sabbath, completely free, without a halter about their mouths or a rope around their necks.

The horse stood waiting when Eli opened the door of the stable. His head was turned half way toward the gate, listening with one ear cocked, the other flattened against his face. His black moist eyes were on Eli, watching him intently.

"Good Sabbath to you, Chestnut," said Eli as he beckoned the horse with his finger. The brown horse answered him with a nod of his head, and both walked out of the stable.

Eli walked ahead, hands clasped behind him. The horse followed in his steps, head bowed low.

The little town under the hot Sabbath sun seemed deserted. Not a soul was to be seen. The doors of the stores were closed and the workshops shut. A dreamy cadence of song was the only sound to be heard. It floated as a whisper through the open windows of little houses. Inside were Jews still sitting around their tables singing the Sabbath hymns. The entire town was covered with a mantle of such glowing warmth and contentment that it seemed as if all of nature were at rest in the peace and quiet of the Sabbath.

In the field, the teamsters of the town lay relaxed and asleep on the soft grass. Their heads rested on their fists, faces up towards the sky. Their horses stood nearby with their eyes half closed, idly plucking the grass and swatting flies from their bodies with their tails. They cat-napped from time to time, standing upright.

Eli also stretched out flat on his back, fists behind his head. He gazed at the small golden clouds that hung motionless in the frame of blue. Delicate tinkling sounds fell like rain from the heavens above and filled the air with crystal bells. "They say it is the song of the skylarks, but where can they be? I do not see a bird in the air. Maybe they are sitting perched on the golden clouds," thought Eli as he closed his eyes.

Suddenly he felt a warm breath gliding across his face and something cool and moist passing over his cheek. Eli opened his eyes and saw Chestnut's head with the big black moist eyes above him.

"Sh . . .," whispered Chestnut in a human voice. "Do not disturb those who are sleeping. Come, get up and we will take a leisurely Sabbath stroll."

"Chestnut, my brown sage," exclaimed Eli. "You have been bewitched. Or has an evil spirit taken possession of you? Whoever heard of a horse talking like a human being!"

"Sh . . . be quiet," again whispered Chestnut in his ear. "You ought to be ashamed of yourself. You, a student who has studied the Bible, does not remember that Balaam's donkey talked like a man."

"Well, what do you know? You are quite a scholar! Where did you learn all that?" asked Eli.

"We animals speak very seldom. But we listen a lot. And if you listen more than you talk, you learn a lot," explained Chestnut. "And now, Eli, my friend, get up on my back and we will make a journey through the Sabbath."

"Chestnut, you know that I am not allowed to ride you on the Sabbath."

"Yes, that is true. You cannot ride me on the Sabbath when you put a saddle on my back and a halter about my mouth and take a whip in your hand. This time I am asking you to ride on me for fun. It is like a game boys play when one carries the other piggy back. This is allowed on the Sabbath."

"But I am afraid someone will see us."

"No one will see us, Eli."

"How far do you wish to go, Chestnut?"

"Very far."

"But on the Sabbath we must not walk too far," Eli warned.

"That is right, Eli. We will not walk. It will come to us."

"That cannot be."

"It can be, Eli. Do you remember the winter when I flew with your sled across the snow? You sat in the sled and you thought that the houses, the trees and the telegraph poles were running towards you and that the sled was standing still. And yesterday, when you longed to see your brother Moses who is in America, you did see America in your dream. Did you go to New York, or did New York come to you? Well, now, come along, Eli, quickly. Hop on my back and—swish. . . ."

And instantly Eli saw cities, countries, rivers, mountains and oceans fly past him. He saw the green fields of summer, then autumn, winter and spring. Everything flew past him with the speed of lightning. Gradually things slowed down and Eli noticed, looming on the distant horizon, a most wondrous gate.

It grew taller and gleamed with the colors of the rainbow. An immense garden could be seen through the doors of this gate. The garden was radiant with such brilliance as though it were lighted by seven suns hanging from the trees. At last they stopped before the gate and Eli and Chestnut entered the garden.

It was an enchanted garden filled with the most beautiful trees, all heavily laden with sweet fruits. All manner of birds with the most colorful feathers sat in the trees singing sweetly. There were grassy spots between the trunks of the trees on which wolves and sheep, tigers and gazelles, lions and buffaloes, foxes and hares—all grazed together. Calmly and peacefully they chewed the grass and ate the fruits that fell from the trees.

"Where are we?" Eli asked in amazement.

"This, Eli, is the first Sabbath in the Garden of Eden," replied Chestnut. "This is the Sabbath after the first six days in which God created the earth and all that lives on it."

"I know," said Eli. ". . . 'And peace reigned over all the world.' But soon after that, man broke God's commandment and was driven from the Garden of Eden, condemned to hard labor. And ever since man has always slaved and has had not an hour of rest."

"And now we fly back, hold on tight to my mane."

Mountains, valleys, rivers, oceans and countries disappeared quickly behind the horizon.

Suddenly Eli saw from a distance a very wide river, and floating upon it a great many barges laden with large square-cut blocks of sandstone. Thousands of bare-chested men were pulling the barges towards the shore with ropes. They piled the stones upon platforms resting on round wooden poles.

Many other thousands of bare-chested men pulled on ropes and dragged the stones on land toward a gigantic triangular construction.

"Oh, I know," said Eli, "we are now in Egypt and these people are the Hebrews."

As he said this, they came upon a tired, dejected group of men, sitting and eating their bread beneath the searing sun.

"Just one free day a week," one of them groaned, "One free day to rest and see my wife and children, from sunrise to sundown. Now I slave all my life, with death my only hope for freedom."

"One free day a week," repeated the others, "Free from labor, free from the master, free from the whip."

"Yes, one free day a week for all," said one, "But not only for the men, but for the oxen, the horses and all who work for men."

"This is the first time that anyone speaks about us animals," murmured Chestnut, "This is the first time that our rest is considered along with man's."

And before Eli could look around, a mountain flew towards them, wrapped in fire and smoke. A great mass of people was milling around it, and to the accompaniment of thunder and lightning, a mighty voice called out:

"Remember the Sabbath to keep it holy. Six days shalt thou labor and do all thy work, but on the seventh day is a Sabbath unto the Lord, thy God. On it thou shalt not do any work; thou, nor thy son, nor thy daughter; thy man servant nor thy maid servant, nor thy cattle nor thy stranger that is within thy gate. For in six days the Lord made heaven and earth, the sea and all that is therein and rested on the seventh day. Wherefore the Lord blessed the Sabbath day and made it holy."

Eli only heard the last word and the echo of thunder. They continued back on their homeward flight. Behind them rolled lands and mountains, valleys and rivers and oceans. Nations flew quickly past as they sped by. Everywhere they flew and wherever they looked they could see men and the beasts that lived with them, at peace and at rest.

"The Sabbath seems to be observed everywhere in the same way," remarked Eli.

"Yes," said Chestnut. "Not on the same day, however. For Mohammedan's, Friday is their day of rest. Jews observe Saturday and Christians rest on Sunday. But the day on which a rest is observed does not matter. The important thing is that everyone does rest one day during the week. The thunder from the burning mount has reached all the peoples of the world."

"But I see that everyone rests at the same time," Eli commented.

"That is because we are flying with the speed of sound. We fly so fast that a whole week is merely a second," explained Chestnut.

"Chestnut, why have you taken me on this journey?" Eli wondered.

"Because I love you, Eli. On the Sabbath we are both alike before God in the matter of rest, and I am allowed to talk to you. Hold on tight, now. ZZZttt...."

Eli opened his eyes, rubbed them and looked about him. The sun was nodding towards the west and lengthening shadows stretched from the trees. From the forest beyond the horizon a black cloud approached. It was heavy with thunder and lightning and the din of their echo reached Eli's ears.

Chestnut was lying near him, watching him with his big black eyes. Eli thought they were smiling at him.

Eli's father was coming towards them from the little bridge across the stream. He was calling, "Eli, you have fallen asleep and forgotten about the flight of time. It is now time to eat the last meal of Sabbath. Come, we are all waiting for you."

Eli got up. The teamsters and their horses had already left. Only Chestnut and he had remained. They walked together. Chestnut put his head on Eli's shoulder. "Don't worry, Chestnut," Eli assured him. "This will be our secret. I will tell no one about our journey through the Sabbath."

The Miracle of the Echo

HAVE you ever walked among cliffs or by the shore of a woodland lake in the still of the night when the air is so fresh and clear? If you have, you must have shouted a word or sang a tune. Immediately someone from the hilltop or the depth of the woods answered with the sound of your own voice. This is known as an "Echo."

There are, however, echoes, most remarkable echoes, that do not reply immediately. They vanish somewhere far, far into space. Years and years may pass before they return and when they do return one may not even recognize the voice as his own. But when one hears it, a wonderful miracle happens to him, just as it did to a young cantor in a little Jewish town in Lithuania.

In this small town once lived a cantor who had a magnificent voice. He was famed for his singing throughout the country and Jews from all parts of the land came to the old synagogue on the High Holy Days in order to hear him sing.

The cantor had a son whose voice was even more melodious than his father's. Very often the father stepped aside and permitted his son to take his place in the synagogue. The congregation had already resolved that when the time came and the old cantor would no longer be able to plead for them before God, his son would take his place.

While visiting this little town, two influential merchants from the capital city attended Sabbath services in the old synagogue. They heard the young cantor sing and were very impressed. After services were over they approached the old cantor and his son and thanked them heartily for the pleasure they had given them by their singing.

"A young man with a voice like his," said one of the merchants, "should be in our big city. We have a famous conservatory of music and a fine opera theatre. Your son could become world famous."

"Yes," said the old man, "I have heard about that. But our family has been blessed with this God-given gift for generations so that we may stand before Him to sing of the sorrows, the prayers and the hopes of the whole congregation and sing His praises. This to us, is more precious than all the acclaim in the world that an opera star might receive."

This was how the old man felt. His son, however, had different thoughts. One warm spring day soon after Passover, the young man went for a walk in the woods and never returned. Fearing that he might have gotten lost in the dense forest, search parties were organized to look for him. But there was no trace of him. He could not be found. The young man had disappeared as though the earth had swallowed him.

Even as his mother and father and the congregation mourned him as if he were dead, the young man reached the big city the merchants had mentioned and enrolled in the famous conservatory of music. But he failed there. Soon after he entered the school he associated himself with undesirable companions. He spent night after night drinking with them at various bars until he was compelled to leave the conservatory.

After leaving the school he became a wandering minstrel traveling about the estates of the rich Polish gentry. He sang at their weddings and their parties.

Traveling about in this manner, he was once invited to sing at the castle of the Polish count who owned the town where he was born. The singer had to pass through this little town in order to get to the palace.

It was the evening before Yom Kippur. It was a mild evening. The sun had gone, and in passing had brushed the windows of the old synagogue with fire. The town seemed lifeless. Doors and windows were shut. Everybody was in the synagogue.

The young man was overcome by the terrible pain of homesickness as he was being driven through the town. When they reached the far end of town, he asked the coachman to stop and he went into a Polish tavern. The tavern was dimly lit by only one small night lamp. The young singer made his way to a table in the corner and ordered a drink.

As soon as his eyes became accustomed to the dimly lighted room, he noticed Wolf, the town informer, sitting at another table. This man was feared by every Jew in town. Every day he invented different accusations against the Jews and ran to inform on them to the count. The count would then impose heavy fines against the community.

"Wolf," exclaimed the singer, laughing bitterly, "I see you are now the only one in town who is not at the synagogue."

"And you are another," remarked Wolf. "If I were not afraid of the count, I would go into town and tell all the Jews that their long-lost cantor turned up at Yahneck's bar."

"Thanks a lot," said the young man. "Come over here and let's both have a drink."

"Is your voice still so beautiful?" asked Wolf, the informer.

"Certainly," the singer assured him. "It certainly is."

"Well, then, prove it. Sing 'Kol Nidre' for me," insisted Wolf.

The singer closed his eyes. In his mind he saw his mother and father. He recalled his childhood, and forgetting all else, started to sing "Kol Nidre." He sang it beautifully and meaningfully, as if he were singing for the congregation in the synagogue. When he finished, he opened his eyes and saw that the chair where Wolf had sat was empty.

"Where is Wolf?" he asked the Polish bartender.

"The devil only knows!" Yahneck replied. "While you were singing your Jewish hymn, Wolf suddenly burst into tears and ran out."

The young man left the tavern. He seated himself in the carriage and ordered the driver to get out of town as quickly as possible.

Not too long after that the young singer lost his voice. He no longer was welcomed at the estates of the rich gentry, and he began singing in bars and at carnivals.

And so he wandered from town to town, on foot and with a pack upon his back until one day he lost his way in an immense forest.

It was late in autumn and for two days he trudged about without being able to find a footpath or a trail. The only food he had to eat were the late berries that still grew between the mosses, raw mushrooms and half rotten wild apples that had fallen from the trees.

On the third day, footsore and weary, he sat down to rest on the stump of a tree. Not knowing what he was doing, he started to sing "Kol Nidre" with his hoarse voice. The stillness in the woods was so complete that one could hear the quiver of a leaf as it glided to earth on the bark of a tree. Suddenly the stillness was broken. From out of the forest came a most beautiful young voice repeating every word he had just sung. He raised his head in amazement and listened.

"No," he thought, "that cannot be the echo of my voice. It must be some other Jew like myself, walking and singing." Rising from the stump of the tree, he followed the sound of the echo. As soon as he stopped singing, the echo vanished. He started to sing again, and again, from the distance came the young resonant voice in answer—now from the right and now from the left, until he was out of the forest and on a broad highway.

When the melody was ended and the echo from the depths of the forest behind him finished the last note, the former young cantor recognized the voice as his own of so long ago. He recalled the scene in the tavern when he sang "Kol Nidre" the last time, for the informer.

The singer lifted his eyes from the ground and saw a small Jewish town in the distance, with low frame dwellings. High above these little houses rose the synagogue, bathed in the radiance of the late afternoon sun. And every window in the synagogue sparkled in the distance like jewels in settings of liquid gold.

Once again it was the day before Yom Kippur. The town was preparing for the Holy Day. Candles had already been kindled in homes and the street leading to the synagogue was filled with Jews in their white robes. The former cantor remained standing in the middle of the street as an alien, an outcast, not knowing where to turn. Suddenly he felt a hand upon his shoulder and a familiar voice call him by name. He turned and saw that it was Wolf, the informer, and with him were several other Jews.

"Moses," cried Wolf as he embraced him. "I have waited three long years for you. I knew you would come to me. It was you who led me back to God with your singing that night in the tavern. You are my guest. You will sing in our synagogue to-day."

"Wolf," pleaded the cantor, "I cannot sing. I am sick. I have lost my voice."

"You will find your voice again and you will sing," promised Wolf.

The young cantor allowed himself to be led by Wolf. He never uttered a word—not even when Wolf put the robe and the Tallith on him.

The whole community was assembled in the synagogue when they arrived. The synagogue was aglow with light. The Holy Ark was open and three Jews, dressed in white and holding the Holy Scrolls, stood waiting for him, the Cantor. He appoached the altar with his eyes closed. Suddenly he again heard the echo. The miracle had happened! The young cantor began singing "Kol Nidre" with the vibrant and magnificent voice that had been his so very long ago.

The Ill Fated Mill

AT the far end of town where the
river edges its border, stood the wreck of an old mill. Two millstones, overgrown with tall grass, lay half sunken in the water.
The petrified oak was torn up and covered with moss. A big
weeping willow with its long curls curtained the remains of
some old building. The townsfolk called this ruin "The
Accursed."

Long, long ago, in the very ancient past, the town and the mill was owned by a Polish count. The mill was rented to a Jewish family. For generations, this mill had been operated by the fathers and the sons of this one family, until one day a strange Jew came into town and offered the count more money for the lease.

According to the Law of the Torah, it is forbidden for anyone to take away the means of livelihood from another. The miller accused the strange Jew of breaking this law, and called him to appear before the rabbi. But the stranger refused to come. He paid the count the money and bought the lease. A short time later he came back again and with the help of the count's serfs he threw the old miller out of his house.

The dispossessed miller was heartbroken and his eyes were filled with tears as he walked away from the house. In a voice choked with emotion, he said, "May your mill grind and grind, but may you never see the flour."

Several weeks passed. Late one night a big wagon drawn by two black horses drove up to the mill. The wagon was loaded to the top with sacks of corn. A tall peasant wearing a greatcoat of sheepskin, a high fur hat and heavy storm boots, stepped down from the wagon. He walked to the door of the miller's house and knocked. The miller, half asleep, answered the knock and asked the peasant what he wanted.

"I must have the corn in this wagon milled tonight," the peasant told him.

"It is late and the water is now at high tide," said the miller. "Come back tomorrow."

"I must have it today," insisted the peasant. "I will pay you five times as much as you usually get."

The new miller got dressed and taking his lantern, went to the mill. The peasant started to carry his sacks and pour the grain into the funnels. Suddenly the grindstones started to shoot ribbons of fiery sparks. They lighted up the entire mill. The frightened miller ran down to the flour bins, but they were empty.

"The millstones are grinding on the bare stones. They are creating friction," cried the miller.

"It does not matter," the peasant assured him. "I will bring up more sacks of corn."

"You will burn down my mill," shouted the miller.

"I will give you five gold coins for each sack," pleaded the tall peasant, taking out five new gold coins from his pocket.

Blinded by the gold, the miller no longer saw the fiery sparks rising from the grindstones and settling like flies over the whole shadowy mill. The peasant kept bringing sacks of corn and the pockets of the miller bulged with gold.

By the time the peasant brought up his last sack, the mill was completely in flames. The miller barely managed to save his life. He looked about him, and by the light of the fire from his burning mill he saw the peasant standing in the empty wagon, driving his two black horses with a whip and vanishing into the blackness of the night.

When dawn came the mill was in ruins. Shaking with fright, the miller put his hand into his pocket to take out a handful of gold coins, but to his horror he found that his pockets were filled with nothing but black coals. Only then did he remember the last words of the mill's former owner: "May your mill grind and grind, but may you never see any flour."

The Public Billy Goat

IN a little Jewish town there once lived a school teacher who was very poor. His name was Jerochim. He was so poor that he did not even own a goat who would give him milk for his wife and child.

One time the parents of one of his pupils gave him a gift. It was a young nanny goat. Some time later the nanny goat had a little white billy goat.

According to Jewish law, the first-born, if it is a male, belongs to God. This billy goat, therefore, did not belong to Jerochim. Jerochim could neither sell him nor kill him for food. The poor teacher was obliged to raise the billy goat and then let him go free. Such a goat belonged to the entire community and was called a "Public Goat."

Jerochim fed and took care of his little billy goat. When he got bigger he took him to the market place and let him roam. The white little billy goat grew quickly and before long he became a big buck with strong horns and a long white beard. He went from one house to another all day long, eating the grass around the garden fences and the straw from the roofs of the houses. But he never harmed anyone.

However, when the rich money lender took the tools away from a poor shoemaker who owed him some money, the billy goat went to the money lender's home at night and broke all the windows. Another time the goat overturned and spilled a whole sack of flour in the market place during a very busy day. The flour belonged to a shopkeeper who did not give a true measure to his customers.

The poor Jews in town laughed at these antics, but the rich merchants were very displeased. They called a meeting among themselves and determined to give the goat to the grave digger. The goat would then be able to graze on the cemetery grounds.

At that time a huge wild wolf from the nearby forests appeared. He caused a great deal of damage throughout the neighboring villages. He attacked flocks of sheep in broad daylight and snatched away the best sheep. At night he broke into barns and left utter destruction. The count from this area, together with his huntsmen, had been chasing the wolf for weeks, but were unable to track him down.

One summer evening when the town shepherd brought the sheep back from pasture, he told the Jewish sheep owners the most distressing news. He reported that the wolf had grabbed the billy goat from the flock and had run off with him. The Jews were terrified. The community leaders decided to place Jerochim's billy goat at the head of the flock. It was also resolved that everyone should recite psalms all day and beg God to deliver them from the terrible monster.

The following morning the shepherd took the billy goat from the cemetery and placed him at the head of the flock, according to plan.

At sunset, the townswomen left their homes and went out to meet their sheep. Suddenly, through the maze of red dust that covered the sheep they saw Jerochim's billy goat. He was strutting proudly at the head of the flock and between his horns he carried the body of the huge grey wolf.

The story about the wolf and the billy goat quickly spread throughout the entire region. The count and his hunters came into town the next day and begged the Jews to let him have this most remarkable billy goat. But the billy goat had disappeared and no one ever saw him again.

In the Kingdom of the Sabbath Queen

EVERY Jew knows that when the sun goes down on Friday and the first three stars appear in the blue evening sky, the Sabbath Queen comes, bringing with her tranquillity, joy and peace to all men.

Far, far away, beyond the land of Yemen, there once lived a rich and God-fearing Jew whose name was Yisroel. His home was open to all wayfarers and his hand was always ready to help anyone who needed help. His greatest delight, however, was the observance of the Sabbath. All week long he prepared for that day. There was no food that was too good, no fruit too rich, no object too expensive for the Sabbath.

But the wheel of fortune turns. As time went on, Reb Yisroel became poorer and poorer until there came a Friday when there was no bread nor candles in the house with which to greet the Sabbath. Unable to bear the pain of watching his wife and children suffer, Reb Yisroel left his home at dawn while the family slept.

Reb Yisroel wandered half the day through the sands of the desert. At mid-day when the sun was high in the heavens, he reached a chain of mountains that were dark and imposing. There was an opening into a cave and he decided to rest there for the Sabbath.

Yisroel entered the cave and noticed a bright light coming from its recessed depth. He moved closer towards the light and saw that it was an exit leading to a most wonderous green valley. In the valley were fruit-bearing trees and flowers of every description. A palace of white alabaster was in the center of this valley and on its steps stood a beautiful woman. A gold ring with three bright stars encircled her head.

"Welcome to the Land of The Sabbath Queen," the woman greeted Reb Yisroel warmly. She clapped her hands three times and an old man-servant with a white beard appeared. He led Yisroel to a basin filled with clear cold water and after he bathed, the servant dressed him in garments of white silk. Reb Yisroel was then taken to a room that was furnished with a bed and a table. A lighted gold menorah adorned the table which was set with two Hallahs, wine and fine food.

Reb Yisroel welcomed the Sabbath and recited his evening prayers. The attendant returned and served him the food. In the morning Reb Yisroel was awakened by the servant. He was again taken to the basin of fresh water where he washed. After the morning devotions he ate his second meal and took a walk in the green valley.

A blessed peace hovered over the entire valley. Not a leaf stirred. All manner of beast and cattle rested quietly and peaceably in the shadows of the trees. A wolf lay near a lamb; a bear and a cow grazed side by side and antelopes and tigers drank happily from the same spring. Reb Yisroel was filled with a deep and quiet happiness. And thus he spent the whole day in that wonderful green valley.

The attendant came back in the evening and invited Reb Yisroel to eat the third meal of the Sabbath. After the evening prayers Reb Yisroel was led to the palace steps. The beautiful woman, with the three stars in the gold ring about her head, waited for him.

"I know you are my most devoted servant," the woman said to him. "Before you leave my kingdom, I wish to present you with three precious stones. As you see, one is rose colored, another is white and the third is blue. The first stone brings joy; the second, tranquillity; and the third, peace. But remember this: man cannot yet have all three blessings at the same time."

"Oh, Princess," Reb Yisroel exclaimed, "when will your joy, your tranquillity and your peace reign over all the world?"

"When the Messiah comes," answered the beautiful woman.

And immediately everything vanished. Reb Yisroel found himself standing at the gates of a big city.

When Reb Yisroel entered the city, he noticed that all the inhabitants were very sad. He asked why they were so sad and was told that their king had been suffering from melancholia for many years and had forbidden anyone to be happy.

"Take me to him," requested Reb Yisroel. "I will cure his depression." Reb Yisroel was brought before the king and he touched him with the rose colored stone. The king became well and happy again and recalled the command of gloom throughout the land.

The king was very grateful and gave Reb Yisroel a great deal of gold and silver. After a while Yisroel left this city and came to another town.

The people in this town were in a rebellious mood. The king suffered from insomnia and was unable to sleep either by day or night. He forced his subjects to work continuously without any rest. Reb Yisroel touched the king with the white stone and the king became calm and relaxed. He was freed from his restlessness and withdrew the laws of work without rest.

Reb Yisroel traveled on and came to a third city. Here all roads were jammed with soldiers and everyone lived in fear. This king wished to conquer the whole world and was constantly at war. Reb Yisroel touched the king with the blue stone and the king made peace with his neighbors. He disarmed his soldiers and for three days his nation joyfully celebrated the Holiday of Peace.

Reb Yisroel returned to his home town with the many gifts he had received from everyone. He built a palace in the center of an immense garden and this palace was always open to all travelers and to all who were in need. And Reb Yisroel observed the Sabbath with even more dedication, with even greater love and devotion until the end of his days.

The Story of an Old Siddur

THERE was once an old, old prayer book. It was bound in thick brown leather and had big gold letters on the front cover and on the back binding. That was how it had looked a hundred and fifty years ago in Russia when it was presented to a young woman as a wedding gift.

In the course of time the Siddur got old. It lost its front cover and the big gold letters on the binding faded. But the pages were firm and whole, in spite of the many loving hands that had turned them. Some of the pages were stained, but those were stains of tears.

Although the Siddur was old and faded, it was very proud of itself. "I am not just a prayer book." thought the Siddur, "for the history of five generations of a family is recorded on my pages. The life story of every member of the family can be found on these pages—when he was born, when he married and when he died."

A young woman had brought this Siddur with her when she came to America with her husband fifty years ago. It was the most cherished remembrance she had of her mother. For fifty years this prayer book was her confidant and her comfort.

The years flew by. The woman had three sons. Her husband died. The sons married, prospered and each moved to a different corner of this broad land. The woman remained alone with her Siddur in a small apartment in the old Jewish quarter on the East Side of New York.

When the lonely old woman became ill, her neighbors, who loved her, took her to a hospital where she could be cared for. Her Siddur, together with other old papers remained in a corner of a room, forsaken. After a time the janitor of the house came with some other men and removed everything from the vacant apartment. The Siddur and the other papers were placed outside near the garbage cans.

It was during one of those long winter evenings that the poor old Siddur found itself in the street near a pile of old newspapers, empty cartons and other useless articles.

"This is my thanks for a hundred and fifty years of devotion," the Siddur remarked bitterly. "Five generations treasured me, and now I, together with them, have been thrown out into the street."

"Don't complain," said yesterday's newspaper that was lying near it. "One hundred and fifty years is a great age for printed matter. We are discarded on the morrow, a day after we have been read."

"How can you compare yourself to me?" questioned the Siddur haughtily. "That which is printed on my pages is almost three thousand years old. Generation after generation has read my print every single day, even though they know each and every word by memory."

At these words, a thick magazine lying on a garbage can spoke up. "You were set and printed by perhaps three or four people. Five hundred people and huge machines were used in setting me up. The company that published me is a million dollar corporation and is the largest publishing house in the city. Yet, you see where I lie. These are different times."

An icy wind began to blow and the Siddur's pages shivered in the cold.

"Don't shiver," yesterday's newspaper spoke with ironic authority. "You will be quite warm before long."

Later, darkness descended and the old slum was veiled in fog. A gang of Jewish, Irish and Italian boys appeared on the street. They set fire to the old newspapers and cartons that were piled in front of the houses. A big fire was started directly across the house where the Siddur was lying. Sparks, like fireflies flew all about and the flames in the night colored the tenements in red.

"Bring more papers," called one of the gang. Several boys dashed across the street.

"This should burn a long time," declared an Italian boy as he picked up the Siddur.

"Oh, God have mercy on me," implored the Siddur with every prayer in its pages. "Did I have to live a hundred and fifty years to be burned like paper in a heap of trash?"

"Stop!" Another boy grabbed the hand of the Italian. "This is one of our holy prayer books. We must not burn it."

"I am sorry," the Italian boy apologized. "I did not know. Here, take it if you wish."

The Jewish boy wiped the dust from the Siddur with his sleeve and took it to the small synagogue near by. He placed it in the bookcase among the other volumes.

"Whew!" The Siddur took a long, deep breath and moved closer to an old Gemorah.

"You have been rescued from fire?" the Gemorah asked.

"How did you know?" The Siddur was surprised.

"Ah, yes," the Gemorah replied. "Every one of us has come here from such danger."

"Tick, tock, tick, tock," philosophically commented the old clock that hung above the bookcase. "Times change, and so do people."

"You have nothing to fear," the old Gemorah reassured the frightened Siddur. "You are quite safe here."

"Tick, tock, tick, tock," the old clock added, "the worst that can happen to you is that you will be transferred to a big library. There you will be able to sleep in peace another hundred and fifty years."

And the Siddur dozed in the dusky stillness of the synagogue, lulled by its memories of long ago.

Fate, however, did not permit it to sleep too long. One sunny afternoon in May a luxurious limousine stopped in front of the little synagogue. A tall handsome young man, with a thoughtful expression on his face, stepped out of the limousine and walked into the synagogue. He stopped before an old Jew with a white beard who was sitting near the window, absorbed in a book.

"Excuse me for disturbing you," said the young man. "There was an old woman by the name of Rachel Rabinowich in this neighborhood. She died, I understand."

The words awakened the Siddur. It nudged the Gemorah quietly. "That was my mistress," it whispered excitedly. "They are looking for me!"

The old man raised his head from the book. He pushed his eyeglasses onto his forehead and gazed gently at the young stranger.

"Rachel Rabinowich," the old man repeated sadly. "Of course. Who did not know her? She was a saint. But what is it you wish to know about her?"

The young man lowered his head. "What I am looking for now is an old family prayer book that she had. She was my grandmother. Father said that the history of our family was recorded in that prayer book."

"Oh, if only I could shout, call, or speak!" wailed the old Siddur in the bookcase.

"Unfortunately, we can talk only when people read us or study us," observed the old Gemorah. "We are speechless otherwise."

"I can offer you no assurance that the Siddur is here," the old man told the stranger. "So many of our great and important books have been burnt. Occasionally Jewish children find these books and bring them here. Look in the bookcase."

The young man walked towards the bookcase. "Can you read the Holy Tongue?" inquired the old man.

"Yes," the young man replied modestly. "I am a teacher of Oriental languages, specializing in Hebrew."

The Siddur could hardly restrain itself. When the young man started to look through the books in the case, the Siddur became so excited that it fell to the floor.

The young man picked it up carefully and broodingly started to leaf through the pages. He stopped suddenly. "I have found it!" he exclaimed.

"Your grandmother was a very lucky woman," said the old man thoughtfully. "It is not every grandmother that can find her grandchildren."

A new life then began for the old Siddur. Encased in a new leather binding with big letters of gold, it now stands in a place of honor in a large library. Among the numerous names on its old pages another name has been added, written in a true and loving hand:

> *"Today on this day of this month and this year,*
> *a daughter was 'orn to me and she has been*
> *given the name of Rachel."*